WHITE SPAWN

WHITE SPAWN

Marc Laidlaw

WHITE SPAWN Copyright © 2015 Marc Laidlaw
COVER ART Copyright © 2015 François Thisdale

Published in October 2015 by PS Publishing Ltd. by arrangement with the author. All rights reserved by the author. The right of Marc Laidlaw to be identified as Author of this Work has been asserted by him in accordance with the Copyright, Designs and Patents Act 1988.

First Edition

ISBN
978-1-84863-934-8 (Signed Edition)
978-1-84863-933-1

This book is a work of fiction. Names, characters, places and incidents either are products of the author's imagination or are used fictitiously. Any resemblance to actual events or locales or persons, living or dead, is entirely coincidental.

Design and layout by Alligator Tree Graphics.
Printed in Great Britain by TJ International Ltd, Padstow, Cornwall

PS Publishing Ltd / Grosvenor House / 1 New Road /
Hornsea, HU18 1PG / England

editor@pspublishing.co.uk / www.pspublishing.co.uk

For My Daughters

WHITE SPAWN

1

With the river's commands still purling in his ears, he rose from the edge of the pool. As dawn troubled the treetops, he made his way over rounded river rocks until these gave way to mud-sand littered with needles, shot through with fireweed, and the rocks grew sharp among grasping roots and sloughed cedar scales. The trailer's porch light still shone brighter than the sun as he climbed the flimsy aluminum steps and went in. He ran a comb through his wet hair, pulled a bit of moss from the teeth. He dabbed his palms with aftershave, although he hadn't shaved, and slapped it on his neck, then pulled underclothes from the drawer and struggled into them, there between the narrow walls and a bed that, although a jumble, had not been slept in. Over the thin white garments, from a tiny closet, he dragged on the plain beige uniform and fit his feet into hard black uncomfortable shoes. Finally he uncoiled his belt from the shelf in the closet and strapped it on. The gun was already in the holster.

As a false promise of brightness flushed through the woods, he flicked the porch light off and stepped out of the trailer, digging into his pocket for the reassurance of keys, wallet, coins. The white truck seemed to glow up ahead, despite the black haze of mold and crusted pollen that mottled it like a lichenous old stone. It took its time starting; it was cold, which he understood completely. He wondered if it was as numb as his mind, if it knew how it was being steered as he drove it down the rutted dirt road, between a pair of metal posts with their length of chain and *No Trespassing* sign stretched out slack across the gravel. It all changed to asphalt as he hit the county road. The truck began to climb, its rear tires slewing as it took the curves that wound steeply up the side of the river-gouged canyon, still in deep woods, still in the perpetual gloom that noon itself did little to dispel. And noon was far off—almost unimaginable.

At the top of the ridge, the road leveled to follow the crest. Down in green darkness, the river tracked the spine of the ridge, keeping him in reach. He knew that if he turned off the engine, he could have heard it, but he kept going. Past steep drives, past yards hacked out of woods to liberate a bit of lawn, scattered with play sets and vehicles. Some of the cars were even darker than his truck, under the patina of mildew and wood mold, but a few were glossy and shiny, as if freshly waxed and parked in some covered lot away from the elements. Houses with vast glass glaring faces gave the first evidence that the sun had lofted some horizon, somewhere. The road doubled, and suddenly out of nowhere he had company. A traffic intersection with farm trucks idling at crosswalks, spewing fumes. An overpass loomed ahead but he ignored the onramp, hewing to a less frequented road, one that took him over the river again on a rumbling metal bridge. With the river on his other side now, he passed a market, not yet open. A small shack sided in cedar shingles sold coffee to sleepy motorists. He drove past a darkened tavern, a lone Harley leaning against the wall as if it had woken up drunk. The river canyon widened again and again, making way for a four-lane road, wide pastures green in glimpses through the thinning trees. A net was strung among the trunks, straining the sky for whatever traveled there. Golf carts parked in rows. A flash of river in a concrete culvert. Where the valley bottlenecked, houses clustered all over its narrowing walls; an apron of cemented earth spread out treeless, made fallow for developments to come. He passed the entrances of the latest homesteads: River Shores, Woodstream, Mountain Creek. New cars poured through security gates. The white truck kept to itself, even as it joined the rush out of the valley.

For a moment he was over the river again—he could feel it beneath him, channeled under the road, confined in a concrete tunnel men had made. Its whisper was muted but somehow he could hear it. Then its voice, its presence, redoubled as it emerged on the far side of the highway. He couldn't see it, but he sensed its joy at finally breaking free, wending toward the lake beyond a sprawl of strip malls, while his journey took him sharply away from it. Off course. He felt a pang at leaving the river behind. But it wouldn't be for long this time. He wasn't going far.

Four lanes now, and traffic, crawling. He was a speck on a curving off-ramp that folded over and under itself like a fisherman's knot that snared them all. Rain was waiting when he finally cleared the last underpass to speed down a highway suddenly steaming. Trucks floated through the mist, passing like whales barely seen through murky seas. He gripped the wheel and felt the truck shimmy on balding tires, thought about how the slightest move, whether deliberate or in error, would end the same way: with the truck smashing and sliding off the road, taking a dozen other cars with it—possibly more if he veered into oncoming traffic. Surviving in the rush of so many blind, swiftly moving hulks always seemed like a miracle. On and on they raced, pushing and testing the limits of the lanes, the whole world narrowed down to this competitive urge to nose ahead of a car driven by someone you had never seen before and never would again. To pull ahead of the next guy, to reach your destination a fraction of a second before some stranger, became the focus of existence. It should have been no surprise how quickly the exit appeared, and he veered off. Having beaten uncounted others, he found himself suddenly alone.

He drifted toward the city center, past strips of secondhand clothing stores, pawnshops, bail bondsmen. The old train station was a mall now, its benches lined with latte drinkers waiting for shops to open. Across from the Station Mall was the courthouse, where ordinarily he steered into employee parking. On this morning, he turned into the shopping mall lot and parked where he could see the judicial compound across the street. The high walls of the jail yard faced the mall like a sullen challenge. Criminals who had robbed the mall were often penned up in plain sight of it.

He left the truck unlocked. On foot, he crossed the street.

The things that were said to him were the same things he always heard as he checked in and made his way through the offices and hallways to the rotunda; he replied to the usual round of morning greetings without hearing himself. Behind the metal detectors, through the bailiff corridors, out onto a curved balcony that overlooked the round marble floor with its mosaic of the state seal. Sunshine warmed the room, glowing through a stained glass dome that faked a view of lofty evergreens. But it was nothing like the woods; the sharp edges and bright colors turned his stomach, stabbed his eyes.

A jury filed past him into a courtroom. Another dozen citizens waited in a line along the curved railing, waiting for instructions. He walked to a pair of doors beyond them and stepped through.

Court was in session. The judge gave him hardly a glance, the bailiff a slightly longer one before returning to her notes. The jurors were intent, or feigning concentration, on instructions from the judge. The public defense attorney was a young woman in an angular skirt suit. She carried papers to the judge and returned to her table. Another long interval ticked past. Finally the judge muttered inaudibly to the bailiff, who went out through the door at the back of the courtroom. A moment later she returned, leading a very old man in an orange jumpsuit, flanked by two officers.

The jury, as a group, flinched when they saw the old man. Cheeks riddled with sores, forehead oozing blood from a huge abrasion, scabbed lips and eyes caked with hardened pus, hair full of flakes, scalp covered with scabs and weeping sores under close-cut grey stubble.

They watched with varying attempts to hide horror or disgust as the officers led the old man to a seat beside the public defender. The guards stepped back. The lawyer leaned over to whisper to the prisoner. The jurors were finally interested in the proceedings, while the officers were relaxed, bored by the routine.

No one noticed him until he had come all the way down the aisle and stepped up to the defense table, pushing in between the prisoner and the attorney. He had his gun at the old man's head before anyone could react, was pulling him to his feet by the collar of the orange jumpsuit.

"Don't move or he's dead," he said.

The bailiff froze, staring at him as if she hadn't seen him every day for five years. His fellow officers looked just as shocked. None of them reached for a weapon; he thought he saw a cousin to sympathy in their eyes. It was clear they had no idea why he was doing this, but he was careful not to threaten one of them. The prisoner was a stranger to them, after all. They would infer he was engaged in some vendetta. That moment, their doubt, was all he needed.

He had, without thinking consciously, figured it out pretty well.

The sick man gave out a dry rasp, choked by the collar cutting into his throat. The two of them moved together, backward through the courtroom doors, out onto the railed balcony above the rotunda. The jurors were gone. A few visitors were filing into a clerk's office. Intent on their own grievances, they didn't notice what was happening until the other officers came out after him. At that point, someone screamed.

He ducked out of sight, taking the stairs to the ground floor. He tried to give the old man a reassuring look in the moment they were unobserved, switching directions on the landing, but there was nothing like recognition left in those eyes. Not much of anything there. The grizzled mouth was gnarled and narrow, the jutting underjaw swiping at him like a hook, its few teeth tobacco-stained and reeking. Terrible. But as they left the stairs and stepped out into the open rotunda, he had to hide any show of concern and just keep the gun fixed on his hostage.

The other guards were ready for him now. He counted on them to refrain from firing on one of their own. He knew none of them well, so it all came down to the uniform. Either his plan was working or in a crowded courthouse too much was at stake for any one of them to risk it. He kept his weapon on the prisoner's bony temple and walked him toward the main doors, through which he could see straight across the street to the mall parking lot. They were almost clear. Then, as he put his back to the door and pivoted to pull the prisoner after him, someone, some idiot, for no good reason, fired.

He was already carrying much of his prisoner's weight as they swung through the doors and out into the rain, but something in the old man's posture changed. He found himself pulling a figure suddenly heavier, convulsive. Gasping turned to wheezing. They reached the street. Rush hour traffic had thinned. He staggered across the nearly empty street, kicked through shrubs at the thinly planted margin of the lot. His truck occupied the space nearest the lot exit. Pull the door open. Push the old man in. Only now seeing blood soaking the orange jumpsuit below the abdomen. The leg of the jumpsuit was wet to the knee. He looked back and saw red puddles, diluting as the rain came down, and beyond that the doors of the courthouse thrown open, releasing a swarm of movement. He didn't bother with seatbelts. The engine was still warm and started instantly, and he drove out of the lot.

No one followed or tried to obstruct him as he drove past the courthouse, the jail, police headquarters. An officer of the court, holding a wounded hostage at gunpoint, driving north in light morning traffic—and no pursuit. As the rain intensified, it felt like a conspirator. If he couldn't see them, they couldn't see him, wasn't that right? They had aerial surveillance, patrol cars everywhere. They would be studying his flight by means he couldn't understand. They'd try to outwit him, let him get where he was going and apprehend him there. They had an old address on file for him, a place in town, maybe they would stake it out.

The knotted interchange was almost empty. It unkinked, leaving him on the last straight shot of freeway, a quick couple of miles from the turnoff. When he finally left the highway, dipping down into a green notch, he felt the river singing silver underneath him. A sigh of gratitude got loose as he rejoined his brief erratic path to its ceaseless, steady one. The rain had not let up. He felt sure there were shadows moving in the clouds, and a deep thrumming that reminded him of driving alongside a guardrail with the window down, spokes of vacuum pressure swooping at his ears. Helicopters?

The old man's lap was full of blood. The seat was drenched and it had started dripping to the floor, soaking into oily rags and bunched napkins.

He flinched as a vast net dropped out of the sky, but it was only the golf course again. The way ahead was clear. He thought they must have expected him to stay on the freeway, and hadn't thrown barriers across the road. There were alternate routes if they tried roadblocks, but in the end his options were limited. He kept trying to see the river, sending it entreating glances while carefully avoiding the sight of blood. He had a child's terror that simply looking at the old man would worsen his condition. The truck crossed over the bridge; the road and the river swapped sides.

Not long after that, as his passenger was just beginning to gasp and moan, he passed the last traffic light. It kindly held green for him as he banked hard onto the two-lane road.

The old man opened his eyes as they came out of the curve. For the first time he seemed aware of his surroundings, surfacing out of pain and confusion to see the blackish green of trees, the dense grey muck of cloud. There was gratitude in his eyes—for the escape, for what awaited him if he survived. They splashed through a creek that had burst its banks and spilled out over the road, to swirl around the hooves of a few muddy cows that stood on hillocks like islands in a drowned pasture. The rising water gladdened him.

Foot on the floor, he urged the truck along the ridge, whipping around bends. As they started winding down the last stretch toward the river in the valley, he glimpsed the flare of cruiser lights, heard the whoop of a siren, and clearly saw the cars.

It was an ambush. A patrol car pulled out of a driveway behind him as the truck passed, blocking his retreat. Out here where there were no crowds, no traffic, no innocents or witnesses, they would take him. Ahead, a patrol car and the sheriff's truck were parked across the road. In the rain, he saw troopers hunched behind their doors. He also sensed, rather than saw, the river flashing at him from beyond the men, down in the valley. He tapped the brakes just short of the cars, then pulled hard to the left and went over the edge.

The truck didn't end-over; it kept its wheels mostly on the ground for a good part of the descent. Only when it hit a tree did he lose control. The truck slewed around so the rear went first. His only goal was to stay conscious, and he succeeded, through the tumbling and the crashing and the brutal impact against the rock outcrop that finally stopped the truck. He shook off the delirium of shock, something deep and old taking hold of him now. He discovered that he was crumpled against a cedar, in a kneeling position. By force of habit, he got to his feet, turned back to the truck, and pulled the keys out the steering column, fumbling and instantly dropping them as his fingers went numb. They slithered away down the face of the rock, and he wondered why he had bothered. He would never drive this truck again.

The old man lay half in and half out of the cab, sliding slowly down into a bed of cedar mulch. He was covered in blood and moaning weakly.

He took a few steps on weakened legs without any sense of whether he might have been injured. No shattered bones stopped him at any rate, although something in his gut seemed to tear as he bent and caught the old man over his shoulder. He straightened, balancing him like a sack of sticks, trying to avoid further injury to either of them. He staggered off in a crouch, wincing through the trees, as the radios and shouts of their pursuers finally dared to chase them down the slope.

There would be cops at the trailer, but he didn't need to go there; the woods were dense and would keep them hidden. The weak beat of the old man's sickly heart spoke to the pulse in his own neck, reassuring him they still had time. Humus turned to sand. The rain hardly reached here, but the cedars were dark with water running down their bark, and it was so quiet he could hear the river again. A gift of peace, a promise of fulfillment. He nearly lost his footing on the slippery, rounded stones. He raised his eyes and saw he'd reached the pool.

He lowered the old man gently to the shore and looked him over. The pain-blurred eyes were staring at the trees, and he followed their gaze. Here was the reality pathetically aped by the stained-glass ceiling of the courthouse rotunda—black instead of green, dripping wet, nothing sharp in it anywhere, just a wet mist that melted the edges of things and made them all seem to be of one essence.

He rolled the old man over to face the water, deep and clear and swirling in the pool, trailing the maiden's hair grasses, bubbling and laughing, surging up at them with playful swipes, fringed with soft moss like a carpet, welcoming.

The old man looked worse than ever, with his cheeks sunken and the festering sores raw and pink in the grey light. His eyes wept a dry crust as if they couldn't blink. He opened his mouth to croak out a few words, revealing gums raddled with sores, putrid sockets. He crooked a finger that was little more than a thin curved bone, hooking his abductor's head closer so his rattling whisper might be heard.

Men cried out from the trees. They had pushed beyond the trailer and had found a bloody path. They warned him to drop his weapon, to put his hands up, to spread out flat on the gravel, all of which he did without thought of resisting. They stepped on him, wrenched his arms behind and cuffed him, hauled him painfully back onto his feet. That was the first time he felt the extent of his injuries from the crash. The pain he could finally allow himself to feel drove him to the edge of blackness, and then over it. But not before he looked back at the pool and saw only bloody moss on its verge. Their voices chased him down the long decline into darkness, demanding to know what had he done with the prisoner.

Where's the old man? Where's your hostage? Your prisoner?

He's not any of those things, he thought.

"Don't call him that. He's just my daddy."

2

For the last few miles of the ride home from school, alone at the back of the bus, Kayla watched her cellphone lose its signal until finally it had no connection at all to the rest of the world. Totally cut off from civilization—that's how she knew she was home.

The school bus couldn't handle the hill, so even though she was the last rider, alone for the three or four miles since they'd turned off the highway, she felt self-conscious, embarrassed by the special treatment she received. All the other kids boarded and disembarked in groups, went off laughing and chattering, even if they were tormenting each other. But Kayla, alone, rode the last miles aware of the driver's sullen glances at her in the long rearview mirror. It's not my fault, she wanted to say. It's not my fault you've got to drive the extra miles just for one drop. Instead, she only ever said a soft "Thank you," as she climbed down out of the bus idled at the side of the road, just uphill from the winding descent through the trees and into the valley. The driver never responded with more than a "Yep."

She'd heard several times from other kids that until she moved in, the bus never used to come down this road at all. It hadn't needed to. There were plastic play sets at a few of the houses, though maybe the children there were too young—or already grown. The stubby gray castles and miniature pink cottages were black with mold and tree slime; you couldn't tell if they were a year old or twenty. Things got that look right away out here. Her bike was so blackened that she cringed to touch it—not that there was anywhere to ride around here. The steep road stood in the way of every possible outing.

A chainsaw chewed away at the edges of the silence; it could have come from anywhere in the valley, so it gave a false sense of density, of people nearby. She had seen another kid out here, but never on the bus. Once, she'd seem him on the edge of the road, once glimpsed him through the trees—a shock of white hair. She looked and listened for him now, as she braced each step against the steep descent, feeling unbalanced by her backpack full of textbooks. A slight stumble would have sent her rolling the rest of the way.

Dogs barked from near and far—in fact, there went Samuel Gompers, her own mutt, setting up a rapid series of howling barks as he sensed her approach. The road leveled out in a narrow stub of street, an unpaved cul-de-sac with several unmarked openings that could have been logging roads or fire lanes just as easily as driveways. She passed the chained-up drive with the *No Trespassing* sign across it. Past that, a mossy pair of stone-and-mortar pillars framed a black iron gate, ajar. She slipped between the parted black panels and headed down the long, deeply shaded driveway toward the house. The kennel was off to one side, beyond the spare cars, the boat, the ATV, the motorcycle trailer. Samuel Gompers spotted her and nearly convulsed against the wire fence until she let him out. He calmed immediately—poor guy, alone all day. Together they climbed the steps to the deck, which was on the far side of the house, facing the river.

The house was all wood and glass, and looked painfully raw—the color you see inside a gash of pale wood when a saw blade sinks into an old but living tree. Instead of darkening, like every other wooden thing in the valley, the house seemed to be getting paler, more bleached, and fuzzier with time. She sensed it would always stand out here—angular, awkward, alone.

Through the wide windows, Kayla confirmed the house to be empty. She keyed off the alarm system just inside the back door, then immediately went outside again. She saw no reason to go in or announce her arrival to the silent rooms. She dumped her pack on a redwood picnic table, under the overhang of the chalet roof, then went down the steep back steps, calling Gompers to follow her down to the river.

Why not just go to her room and listen to music, or play a game? The woods, despite everything, were still a source of surprise. They hadn't completely bored her yet. Compared to everything else in her life, they remained unpredictable.

Just as now, when a stench of rotting flesh hit her the moment she set foot on the patchy, pale lawn.

She recoiled, but Gompers bounded forward. It occurred to her that this might be one reason he had been so frantic. She followed in spite of her revulsion, a little bit thrilled. It felt good to push on into some kind of mystery, especially when the alternative was homework.

Beyond the balding patch of grass that marked a desultory attempt at a yard, she stepped among thick cedars and spindly pines, crunching over the brittle cones of each. The soil turned sandy and weedy. Grey chunks of rock lay jumbled up to the water's edge. The river was narrow here, and shallow enough to wade across, not that there was any reason to. The far side was nothing more than a steep eroded dirt bank, topped with a dense line of trees whose roots were exposed, some of them far along in the process of losing their grip and sliding down to the bluff. Soon they'd be snags in the river.

Samuel Gompers trotted upstream, to where the water swept around a bend from an encroachment of cottonwoods, as if coming out of hiding. She called him but he ignored her, sniffing something lodged among the rocks. He rubbed his jaws and throat in whatever it was, then threw himself down and started thrashing about on his back. By the time she reached him, he was on his paws again, looking at her happily. The stench clung to him like part of his pelt.

"Gompers, what are you... Oh, gross!"

She didn't have a leash on him or she would have jerked him away. In the rocks at her feet was a pile of rotting flesh, bright orange with silvery grey mashed into it, shiny flecks flashing with a faint gleam of water and sky. It was a huge fish, dead, with jutting jaw and white gills. Gompers, by rolling in it, had smashed up what was already fairly far gone in that direction. Flies settled back onto the carrion, startled when Gompers went in for another dive.

"No!" she commanded. He settled back obediently but with his disappointment plain.

Now that she knew what to look for, she quickly confirmed that this fish alone could not be held to blame for filling the afternoon with the stench of decay. The shore was littered with them. Flies swarmed wherever they lay. Dead giveaways, she thought, and snickered.

"What's so funny?" said a voice that seemed to come out of the river.

She twisted around, startled out of her humor, and saw a face watching her from the shade of the cottonwoods. It was him, the boy with white hair. He was hunched up, sitting on a boulder. She took a few steps toward him. He was pale and dappled by the trees, in pale yellow shade like camouflage.

"Nothing," she said. "What are you doing in there?"

"Do you think it's funny that they're dying?" he said, as Gompers plunged in among the trees, sniffing around the boy's bare feet, sniffing his legs. The boy's bony hands moved over Gomper's head, between his ears, rubbing the fur the wrong way, just how Gompers liked it.

"Are they salmon?" she asked.

"What else would they be?"

"I don't know. Trout?"

He shook his head and put a finger to his lips, then pointed at the river through the skinny saplings. She went and stood next to him, knelt, followed his finger. The river was at its shallowest here, a rumpled sheet of water stretched over the rocky bed, bubbling in small pools, humping over drowned branches, carrying leaves and debris downstream. It was a clear silver dazzle to her—not even a blur of motion, too transparent for that. Moss streamed from the rocks, which were blue and grey except where the water made them silver. And then a bit of the silver shivered and curled in upon itself, gaining heft and solidity, until with a spasm it launched from the water and came down again onto its other side, settling among fissured edges of rock. Finally she realized she was looking at a fish—enormous, longer than her arm, so fat the flow of water barely covered it. The river, shallow here, coursed over it but offered no transport. It struggled then fell still. It was lucky to have landed in a pool between the rocks and not atop them, where it would have strangled in the air.

"Does that look like a trout to you?"

She had only seen trout in a grocery store, under plastic wrap, and they had been a great deal smaller. She shrugged.

"What's it doing? They swim upriver, don't they?"

She feared he would greet the question with condescension, make her feel stupid for asking, but he only shrugged. "Maybe it's confused."

"Should we help it? It looks stuck."

"It would need a lot of help to get where it's going. The river's like all the way up to the dam. But there's a deep spot, a pool, right around the bend. We could help it get that far at least."

"Pick it up, you mean?"

He stood and stepped into the river, looked back to see if she was coming. Kayla slipped out of her shoes and rolled up her jeans. Together they bent over the struggling salmon.

"Is it...Is it sick?" she asked after inspecting it a moment.

"Sort of looks that way," he said.

Examining it more closely, she thought of the rotting fish Gompers had rolled in. The scaly grey skin was blistered and covered with sores, raw wounds from which shreds of white flesh drifted and clung like feeding parasites. The eyes were filmed over, cloudy, as if the fish had spent too much time out of the water and begun to dry up. The gills looked as if mold had invaded them. She could hardly believe a creature could look this sick and still be alive.

"I know what it is," he said. "They come upstream to die."

He leaned to the water and dug his hands under the salmon. It began thrashing at his touch. She bent across and laid her hands over the top of the fish, though it made her sick to think of touching the diseased flesh. She couldn't believe there were any contagions that spread between fish and humans, but whatever the fish had, illness this intense was terrifying.

They straightened, cradling the creature between them, and as they rose they faltered, staring into each other's eyes. His were silver, the same color as the river—although that was just the grey afternoon light. His hair was wispy, impossibly blond, almost pure white. He was very pale and very skinny, but wiry as well, and strong. Somehow he managed to grip the slimy, struggling fish. Her own grasp on it seemed unneeded. She let go, aware only of the slime that covered her palms. He turned and started upriver, against the current, and she followed close behind.

"If it gets away, I'll grab it," she said.

"We have to hurry, but the pool's not far."

Wading in the icy water, it was tough going. The rocks were slippery and sharp, and the flat ones tipped and tilted when she stepped on them. She was fairly certain she would end up soaked. He moved steadily, water surging around his shins, the salmon hugged to his chest, its head and tail flopping on either side of his narrow frame. It no longer struggled. Weak, dying, it had given up. She felt proud of their rescue attempt, even if it was futile.

"I thought," she said, fighting back gasps with each painfully cold step, feeling the shivering start to come up through her jaws and tensed shoulders, "they came up…upstream to…to spawn."

"They do," he said distractedly. "And that's all they do. Every bit of life they have, they burn it up. That's why they look so sick. There's nothing left to fight off disease. Their bodies don't care if they die, cause they're just going to lay their eggs. Or fertilize them. I don't know if this is male or female. Do you know how to tell?"

"Maybe we should have soaked a shirt and wrapped it up, so it'd have water to breathe while you're carrying it."

"My shirt?" he said with a laugh.

The river twined around another bend, a gravel bank jutting out beyond a thick growth of shrubs and blackberries. There were tire tracks in the gravel, ruts full of water, leading away through the brush into mud. More dead fish here too. The salmon had dashed themselves on the rocks or mistakenly beached on the bank. The flies were thick, the stench worse than ever. But beyond the gravel bar was a wide spot with an unbroken sheen that suggested deep water. It wasn't purling over rocks or shallow fallen logs. The center of the pool was slowly swirling, leaves and bubbles caught in a gyre, defying the powerful flow. The boy skirted the depths, moving along the shore. The opposite side was a steep, heavily eroded bank with trees leaning out so far she couldn't make out the ridgeline above. Although the river widened here, it was darker; the air felt as cold as the water. A chill passed into her heart and held there, like the dark water circling in the pool.

She nearly bumped into him. She'd been working her way around toward the shore, with her eye on the far bank, and hadn't realized he'd stopped.

"Here," he said, holding out the salmon. "You do it."

She had almost gotten away with no further slime, but she couldn't refuse since he had carried it all this way. The poor thing was growing tacky, its gills gaping spasmodically. She found it easier to hold now that it no longer fought, but the full weight of it still surprised her.

Crouching, she lowered the salmon into the stream. Its jaws and gills shuddered and began to pump. Life sprang into it, as if it had been dormant until it sensed the pool. Then with a sinuous silvery flash, the salmon was gone, into the depths, aimed upriver.

He looked at her and put out a slimy, scale-speckled hand. "Good job!"

She hesitated then remembered that she'd been slimed as well. She squeezed his hand and felt the slippery mucus squishing between their palms. It was the river's version of a blood oath.

"What's your name anyway?" she asked. "I'm Kayla."

Before he could answer, the word came out of the afternoon air: "*Thor!* What the hell are you doing there? Haven't you heard I been calling you? I told you not to come down here alone—"

They both turned to where a woman had come out of the brush along the tire path. She was morbidly fat or obese or, as Kayla's mother would have put it, heavy. The woman's hair, years ago, might have looked the same as the boy's—white and soft. Now it was graying and coarse. A wide pale woman, squat as a giant toadstool in the forest gloom, her mouth turned down like that of a huge old frog or bulldog. Her scowl deepened as she squinted past Thor.

"Who's she?" the woman demanded.

"Just a friend," said Thor, already splashing up onto the gravel.

"Well you get up here, I need your help. Been calling all around for you."

"I'd better get back anyway," Kayla said.

Thor gave her a backward look and a wave, then hurried across the gravel, as quick and easy as if he'd been wearing shoes. The woman waited for the boy to go past her into the trees, then gave one last hard look back at the pool. She seemed to stare right through Kayla, with an impersonal glare that might have been meant as a warning to the world in general. Then she was gone.

Kayla waded to the bank and picked her way painfully along the shore to her shoes.

3

"I met that boy today, by the river." Kayla watched her mom shake her head sadly and flick a glance over at Chuck, who was deep into dinner food and didn't notice. "Did you know his name was Thor?"

"That poor boy," her mother said.

"What? Why?"

"Well, his family, you know."

"I don't know. How could I? I didn't ask him anything. We saved a salmon. I saw his mother."

"That couldn't have been his mother, honey. I think he lives with his grandmother, over there somewhere past the old trailer."

Kayla had seen the trailer the weekend she and her mother had moved in with Chuck. He had pointed it out to her, saying, "Don't go around that place. Those people are very particular about boundaries. Even the river, they treat it like it's private property. Probably better you don't go upriver at all. They live all up in there. God knows what they're up to."

But right now Chuck wasn't saying anything. It seemed like his thoughts were elsewhere. Maybe he and her mom were fighting.

Maybe they would break up soon so she could move away from here. In which case it wasn't worth making a friend or knowing anything more about Thor. Except, that was ridiculous. Life wasn't a fairy tale where her wishes would be granted. They never would leave this place. She'd be stuck here with Chuck forever. And as for friends, Thor was the only kid for miles around as far as she could tell.

"She didn't look old enough to be his grandmother," Kayla said. "She wasn't any older than you."

"Thank you so much for that," said her mother. She wiped her mouth, adding extra delicacy to her next words. "Some people just start *earlier* than others."

A few of the things Kayla might have said then, she suppressed. She did not want Chuck telling her to quit the backtalk. Leave him alone and he'd finish eating and leave. So she only said, "I don't think he goes to school. He's not on the bus."

"No, of course not. He's homeschooled."

"Where do you hear these things?" she said. "I never hear anything."

"Down the river, some of the neighbors are very nice. That Thor, they say his father is in jail after some sort of incident, and the mother has been out of the picture for a long time. Maybe she's in jail too."

"For what?"

"Meth," said Chuck with grim satisfaction. "Probably, anyway. That's why I told you not to go upriver. Back in those woods they are bound to be cooking. These places attract that element. Trees keep them hid from aerial surveillance. No neighbors around to smell the stuff. Why do you think I put in the alarm system? They get desperate, or their customers do, they start hitting houses on the edge of the woods."

"But we're way out here in the middle."

"Just don't go past the property line," he said.

"They don't *own* the river."

"Kayla," her mother started, but Chuck had more to say.

"I had one of them pull a gun on me when I first built this house. I was working my way upstream with my rod, came around a bend and he was standing there with a shotgun. At first I thought he was fishing with it! But he turned it on me quick enough. The river's mostly too low for rafters or inner tubes to make their way down from the dam, or I'm sure there would have been some kind of confrontation by now. Some sort of violent confrontation."

"Was it Thor's father? With the gun, I mean?"

"I don't know. This was a couple years back, it could have been. It's all cousins and relations in there. I can't tell a lot of them apart. And that episode didn't exactly make me want to get to know them better."

"Just go downriver," her mother said. "There's nicer people that way."

"People who don't have kids," she said, and then Chuck finished eating and glared at her, daring her to show more resentment. She shut up.

Darkness was complete by the time she'd loaded the dishwasher and cleared the table. Night came early this deep in the valley, and usually it was a night of no stars, clouds clamping down like a lid. She walked toward the river, following the sound through the dark. She looked back at the house, a big glass box full of light. It creeped her out to think that anyone coming down the river could gaze right into their lives. Their privacy was an illusion, based on the belief that no one would ever come by, that nobody could possibly care to look.

She used the crunch of river sand as a guide. As soon as she felt it, she turned and started upriver, her eyes growing steadily more accustomed to the dark. The air was damp, the sort of cold that soaked through her sweatshirt hoodie like ice water. She savored the chill; the coming numbness made her more aware of her body.

The gravel bar had a dull, powder-grey appearance in the dark. It was the palest shape in a blurry black-and-white photograph. As she moved forward, a faint light broke through the screen of trees—just enough to add certainty to her steps. A few paces on and she felt the rutted track underfoot. She was on the path Thor had taken.

Before too long she saw a window, narrow and high, curtained and dim, yellowed as an old parchment lampshade. Like Chuck's house, it was only visible if you came upon it from the river.

She crept closer, the secret trailer emerging from the night. Much of the boxy shape was shadowed, caught in the grip of berry vines. The window was too high for her to look into, so she went around to the side that was free of brambles and put a foot on the metal mesh stair set below the door, still moving in close to perfect silence. The trailer barely shifted as she put her weight onto the step and looked through the curtained window framed by the door.

Thor sat at a small Formica foldout table, bent over books and papers, reading. Her first thought was that homeschool homework looked much like her own. She knocked as quietly as she could, startled when the aluminum door rattled as if she had banged a can full of rocks against it. He jumped, his shocking white hair floating up like dandelion fluff, his white face wild as he spun toward the door.

"It's me!" she said. "It's Kayla!"

He opened the door with shaking hands. "Get in!"

"Sorry if I scared you."

"I thought it was my gramma. I'm not really supposed to be here."

She stood in the middle of the trailer and looked both ways down the narrow aisle, from the curtained-off end to the kitchen nook. The floor was covered with black pellets: mouse droppings. Looking around, she saw them littering most of the surfaces except the benches and the table where Thor was working. The place stank of pee and mildew.

"It's my dad's trailer," he said. "These were his books." He was working by a battery lamp; it didn't give much light, but the trailer was small. "You can look if you want. If you can keep a secret, I'll show you some other stuff too. You haven't been here long, have you? You live in the big house next door?"

"Where is your dad?" she asked, nodding.

"He's on a trip I'm not supposed to talk about. He does stuff for the government even though he really doesn't work for them. It's more like undercover. They won't tell me much about it, my gramma and my uncles. That's one reason I started reading his books. I'm looking for clues."

He pushed one toward her. She saw it was something about myths and legends.

"I think he stayed out here because he could do his work without surveillance."

She remembered what Chuck had said about the whole family hiding in the woods to make drugs. But it didn't seem like Chuck knew the real story, and now she was hearing it.

"The government would eavesdrop and tap his phone, so he didn't have one. He didn't even have a computer. My gramma has one in her house, but I'm not allowed to use it. Do you have a computer?"

She almost said, "Of course," but she realized the rules were different here. Thor was not like the kids at school with their smartphones and tablets, wearing their expensive jeans and trying to impress each other even though all they did was buy the same clothes as everybody else at the same shops in the mall. So she changed the subject to the book, which was full of drawings and art and symbols, Native American totems and carved images of orcas and eagles. It was the stuff you saw in the tourist shops and street fairs in Seattle. Pacific Northwest Indian souvenirs and carvings. Even the casinos, owned and run by Indians, used the pictures in their advertisements.

"Was your dad working with, uh, Native Americans or something? In the government?"

"I think he was just trying to understand the old ways. The *real* old ways. Older than the Indians."

"You're supposed to call them Native Americans," she said, and he put on a distant, patient face.

"They're not really native," he said with authority. "There are older things here. Really, we were the first people. The oldest things were waiting for us all along. That's what Gramma says."

"The natives were here before anybody. That's why they're called natives."

"I'm sorry you believe that, but it's a lie, like everything they teach in school. They were Asians originally, like, from China. They found out about America and came over on the land bridge. But our people were already here, exploring and conquering."

"What people are your people?"

"The pure stock. We were the first. We didn't have to walk, you see."

"You mean, like, Vikings? In their boats?"

"We ruled the water and the land. The gods promised it to us! But while we were making our way, the Indians infiltrated and stole it out from under us. You look at the regular books and all you see is lies. The real truth is always more interesting. The schoolbook history is boring—that's one way you know it's not true. The old world, it's always been ours. And someday we'll take it back. It wants to come back to us. Just look at how much the others have screwed everything up. They weren't good caretakers. They had their chance and they blew it."

"Did your gramma tell you all this?" she asked.

"She wouldn't like if I was talking to you."

"Thor, don't worry. I won't tell."

She thumbed through a few more books. Some of them looked like they were no better than someone's sloppy school report, printed and bound. There were notebooks too, written in a childish hand. She felt a growing embarrassment for Thor. He had no idea how crazy he sounded to an educated person; no idea what the world was really like beyond this valley.

A wind came up and thumped the side of the trailer, and then a pelting rain that sounded like pebbles scattered over the roof. The blackberry hedge dragged its thorns along the window over the table where they sat. She scanned the dim walls outside their circle of light, looking at carved wooden fish, rough-hewn, hung up on tacks. Scattered between them were several equally crude wooden crosses with flared arms of equal length.

"Are you a Nazi?" she asked suddenly.

"I think they're all dead," he said. "And anyhow that was Germany. Do you want to see another secret?"

"I'm not sure you should show me," she said, but he looked so crestfallen that she said, "All right."

He got up and opened a little closet in the hall. Some suits that looked like uniforms hung slack from a few wire hangers. He pushed them flat against one wall, then leaned in and pulled up the floor of the closet. It opened on hinges like the lid of a trunk. Earthy air wafted up out of the blackness. There was a collapsible ladder inside that went down about a foot or so but could be lowered farther. Thor held up the lantern so she could see a hatch cover down there, buried so it was flush with the earth, and locked with a heavy padlock.

"What is it?" she asked.

"A hiding place, a supply cache, I'm not sure. I've been looking for the key, and when I find it, I'll know all his secrets."

"You sure are into secrets," she said, watching him lower the floor of the closet back into place.

"Aren't you?"

"I don't have any interesting ones. Only ones I keep from my mom and her boyfriend. They're not big, mysterious secrets like yours. Just the things I think about that would make them mad if they knew."

"I have an idea what my dad's secrets are about anyway," he said. They went back to the table and sat. "Just from what my uncles say, I think they're planning something big. They all used to be in the army, and they still have connections. I've heard them talking about explosives. I think they have stuff hidden somewhere."

"Why are you telling me this? What if I went to the police and got your family in trouble?"

He gave her a puzzled look. "You helped me save the fish. I knew as soon as I saw you that you were the one for me. When you wanted to rescue that poor salmon, I knew I could trust you."

Thor moved closer to her on the bench and ran his hand over hers where it lay on the table, a very light, thrilling touch. She turned her hand palm upward so they could lace fingers. It was the grip they'd had before—holding hands by the pool—but with nothing between them this time, nothing to make her squeamish. Although the things he said sounded crazy, in a way, that was only because of how he'd been brought up, spending his life in this isolated valley with only crazy people telling him what to believe. What he really needed was someone like her in his life. No, not someone *like* her—but Kayla herself, only Kayla, no one else. She thought—she believed—she *knew* she could save him.

His eyes were silver, deep and clear. They hid nothing, held nothing back. Nothing waited inside him to frighten or hurt her. He was all on the surface, she could see every thought in his eyes. And then they were too close to see because she was kissing him, caressing hair soft as down or feathers in her fingers. He gripped her arms just below the shoulders, and his hands didn't move from there, as if he didn't want her to wriggle away. Again, she thought of the salmon, how between them they had saved its life. That was a good thing to have done, a good start. It had created a bond and brought them so quickly together.

But then it all ended with a clamor and a bang, and a woman's shrieks. It was the second time that day she'd heard the voice. Thor's grandmother.

The enormous woman threw open the door, but she looked too large to fit through it. Thor squirmed back into the nook, as if frightened she might reach in and tear him out, like a snail from its shell. There was no getting around the woman, no way out, until Chuck imposed himself between Thor's grandmother and the doorway.

He climbed in quickly, with an expression more harried and fearful than angry.

"You kids, come on out of here. I had to come looking. Kayla, your mom was in a panic. Freya thought the boy was in his room, but when we found you were both missing, she figured you might be down here."

"We're just looking at books," she said. "We're not doing anything wrong."

"You're not to be with him!" the woman said. "Stay away from my Thor!"

The boy gave her a stricken look, getting slowly to his feet. "Gramma..."

"We'll talk when you're home and not before," she said. "Now get down here!"

Thor reached back for the lantern, and used the move to grab Kayla with his other hand, squeezing her fingers.

"I love you," he whispered, and was out.

"Kayla." That was Chuck. "You too."

The rain had stopped, which made the woods seem muffled, empty. She could hear Thor and his grandmother heading off through the trees as she trudged along after Chuck. She thought she heard them murmuring, but realized as the sound refused to fade that it was simply the noise of the river, louder than ever.

"You scared your mother shitless, you know."

"If our phones worked out here, she could have called me."

For once, he didn't take the bait. "I told you those people are freaks. You should think of someone besides yourself for once."

I am, she thought. It was true. Thor's eyes. Thor's lips. How he had held her, and she him; the way they had carried the life of the fish between them, as if they were rescuing each other.

4

Samuel Gompers ran down to the river and was about to kneel and roll in the carrion when she caught him by his collar. Even more salmon in the river this morning, silver in the early light. Later the flies would descend, but for now it was cold, the woods wreathed with mist. The rocky banks had claimed another three or four victims in the night, just along the short stretch that she could see—but the water was alive with free swimmers. After the rain, it seemed to be running deeper. They were no longer hung up in the shallows. Keeping her hopes in check, she looked up the watery track and saw nothing at the bend, no pale face watching from the cottonwoods. As expected. She walked back to the house and grabbed her backpack. Chuck was running his truck, honking at her to hurry. Her mother's car had been gone when she woke up.

She ordered Gompers into his kennel and climbed into the cab next to Chuck. She tried to sound him out about his afternoon plans, without letting on what she was up to. He was still pissed about last night, and wouldn't be drawn into conversation. He'd hardly said a word to her all morning, banging around the kitchen making coffee.

He dropped her at the bus stop, at the top of the hill, and drove off, still without a word. Sour and reserved, he had learned to communicate with looks and never say anything she could repeat.

The school day held one surprise, in the form of a field trip, and it was strange how it slotted into her preoccupations. It seemed like a sequel to her river dreams. The class boarded a bus and went down to the salmon ladder at city center. From the cold plaza swarming with kids, chilly ramps ran down into dank lobbies where glass walls held back the river. On the other side of those walls, salmon teemed in the thousands. Like the one she and Thor had rescued, these were dying as they swam, festering with blisters and chancres and open sores. Spawning season was near its peak, and hatchery personnel were on hand to answer questions few of the children asked. Kayla wasn't sure if the water they swam in was fed by the river that ran past Chuck's house. There was no telling, for this one was channeled under streets, trapped in concrete tunnels, the very soul of it rerouted and diverted for their edification. She already knew what the guide, a skinny old woman in a ranger's hat, would tell them; she tuned out the explanations. Instead she thought about Thor, wanting to get back on the bus, willing it to take her straight home. She was swept up in dying eyes and muscular, writhing bodies, calmed by the gurgling speech of water echoing in concrete chambers. The remainder of the day, the ride back to school and the last couple classes hardly registered.

Thor was waiting in the woods at the back of the yard when she got home. She saw him from the deck, and when she released her grip on Gompers's collar, the dog ran straight to him. After a quick check to make sure no one was home, she ran down the steps to meet him.

After last night it would have been stupid not to hold hands, but beyond that, she wasn't sure what to do or say. She thought about bringing Thor up to the house but there was nothing there she wanted to show him. Her room was just a thin layer of her stuff dumped into a strange place, barely concealing how unlived-in it felt. That situation was too complicated to explain right now, and she didn't want him to pick up on any of it. If they got into talking about her mom and dad and Chuck, she was afraid she'd have to ask about *his* family—which seemed like a topic set with traps. There were dangers around both of them really, like landmines planted all along the edges of a narrow twisting path. It was a path they could safely travel only by walking very close to one another. So for now, they followed the river upstream, fingers interlocked, stepping over salmon that had died on the rocks, sometimes pushing stragglers over shallow stretches of pebbles so they could swim free.

As they hurried past the puddled tire tracks, Thor sensed her nervousness. He said, "Don't worry, she's out all afternoon. But let's not hang around here. I want to show you something."

They went past the pool with its slow, deep gyre and the steep bank of trees hanging over it. On into deeper woods, in and out of sky, from shade to drizzle and a swift blaze of blue sunlight, then back into cloudmurk again. She heard snatches of voices every now and then. It was hard to tell where they came from—how near, how many, or much of anything else. Once she thought she heard Thor whispering to her, but when she looked around she found him gazing at the river. The sound she'd thought was his voice wasn't words at all, but the rippling of the river over stones.

He caught her looking, then tugged her away from the water. "We shouldn't be seen here," he whispered, pulling her into the woods, as if retrieving their reflections from the broad shallow pools. The open sky, mirrored in the river, made her feel vulnerable. She edged closer to him and took comfort from his presence as they trod the very verge of woodland shade. She jumped at an abrupt crack that sounded like a gun going off. Chuck had warned her, in another of his threatening lectures, that there were illegal firing ranges in the valley. But Thor didn't seem worried about getting shot.

"That's just my uncles," he said.

"Don't you have any aunts?"

"Just my grandma. I mean…she's the only lady around right now."

The presence of his uncles was reinforced by occasional glimpses of houses through the trees. Fenced-in compounds and wire pens with nothing in them. Yards littered with cylindrical constructs of chicken wire, lined with black felt roofing paper and filled with cracked plaster or cement. Overgrown piles of plumbing and engine parts and rotting green lumber.

It was all so thrilling to her: The cold air, the sound of silver water always near, the throaty roar of motors ripping to life in the woods. They crept past small shacks, a row of motorcycles. A big house sat at the end of the road. Official vehicles were parked close around it, as if surrounding the house in a siege.

"I think someone's in trouble," she said.

"Naw. Some of my uncles work for the water company. Those are their trucks. The other day I saw a jeep from Fort Clark up here. The army base? Couple of my uncles are stationed there. We just can't let them know what I'm showing you. It's not too much farther."

"Not too much farther" turned out to be fairly far. The river widened, and as it did Thor grew less nervous about walking beside it. The sounds of men receded, but the stench of rotting fish grew worse. The water ran shallower. Here the fish struggled again, as they had downstream.

They entered a stretch where the trees along the river's edge looked like used matchsticks, hacked up and burnt to stubs. Some of the old cedars had been mutilated with chainsaws and axes before being torched. At first it looked like random vandalism, but then she recognized the signs of someone so unhappy with their work that they'd tried to destroy it, like the half-finished craft projects that cluttered her closet, abandoned once she'd realized they couldn't keep her from thinking too much or feeling sorry for herself. Having noticed the first evidence of carving, she began to see it everywhere. Eventually they reached a place where the craftsmen must have been pleased with their efforts and had stopped destroying their work. It was as if lightning had blasted acres of trees, stripping them of bark and branches. Whose hands had whittled these faces and figures into the living wood? It was chainsaw art taken to its highest level, turning out totem poles like none she'd ever seen. Popping eyes, downturned mouths agape, jagged gills. Fish faces were found among Native American carvings of course, but these were done in a style she couldn't place. There were crosses, ravens, runes that might have been Viking or even Elvish for all she knew.

These trees, with their stripped branches, made perfect roosts for feeding birds that waited to drop down and feast on the lost, floundering fish. The river here offered little in the way of sanctuary, and her sense of helplessness deepened. She identified bald eagles, red-tailed hawks, and kestrels perched and waiting. The raptors dived and struck, soared off with struggling silver bodies clenched in their talons. Some landed on the farther shore and fed; others returned to perch among the oppressive totems. The bare branches were draped with shreds of dried grey skin, and the sound of the river was muffled beneath the clacking and cries of the predators.

"It's because the river's too slow and shallow now," Thor said, his eyes full of tears. "It's all been ruined because of the dam. It's out of balance—the birds shouldn't have it so easy. There's no respect for the old ways."

He turned to her and even though they had been holding hands much of the time, he squeezed hers even tighter now. "It should be free again."

"The river?"

"It should run wild."

"Doesn't the dam hold drinking water for the whole area? The city and everything?" A few bits of lecture from the field trip had resurfaced.

"That's what's wrong," he said. "The whole idea that because there are so many people, they can just *take* what should only belong to a few. It isn't right. The city didn't ask—the government didn't ask—nobody asked. They came in and took. Well…" He pushed back a lock of pale fluff. "It doesn't have to be that way. It won't always. You'll see. You're the one for me, Kayla, so you will definitely see."

She grew flushed and her ears began to sing with a high thin sound; she felt giddy and privileged. The carved guardians seemed to lean in, waiting for her response. She put her arms around him and thought how amazing it was that they had met. The sound of the raptors and the stench of carrion faded away; all she heard now was the river and her heartbeat. For the first time, she was able to imagine something positive coming from the events that had brought her here. Her mother always promised things would work out, and Kayla easily dismissed it as a lie, the sort of thing you said to distract a little kid. But she was finding her own way through now, with the help of a friend. Someone who could one day be more than just a friend.

"We're almost there," he said, and she opened her eyes, tugged along even faster. They left the feeding birds and staring trees behind.

"They keep some of the salmon out of the river," she said, coming back to the moment. "I found that out today. Because they would die up here and then rot, they keep them out of the drinking water."

"That's what I'm talking about! Who gives them the right to decide that? It goes against nature."

She wished she had paid more attention at the fish ladder, so she could add to what Thor already knew. She wanted something else that might impress him. But suddenly he pulled her back into the trees. He quietly pointed to a trampled path through dense ferns. It looked fresh, as if others had been here recently.

"We can't take a chance of being seen," he said. "But we can watch from here."

He pointed up through the trees. She saw a slanted grey wall with water sheeting down across its face. Atop the wall was a line of pylons holding up a bridge. The dam let water through at a sluggish pace. It took her a long time to realize how large it was. The concrete wall spanned the river canyon from side to side. There was a small diversion far to the right of the base, where a small stream emptied into the shallows. Thor singled it out as the spot where the fish went through. But it was so puny, especially if you considered how great the river must have been in its primal state.

"Kayla, I think we can bring it back."

"Bring it back how? How do you mean?"

He stepped just far enough out of the trees to point out some structures that topped the left side of the dam. "There's security up there—fences and guards. But my uncles...Like I said, some of them work there. The water company trusts us; we're caretakers now. But that means something different to us."

She squeezed his hand. "What are they going to do?"

He started to speak, but a distant voice arrested him.

"Down!"

He pushed her back and they crouched in the ferns. She saw people, tiny in the distance, moving along the top of the dam.

"Come on," he said. "We can't stay here."

He led them toward the side of the canyon, into the thickest woods. As they made their way along the valley edge, they came upon tire tracks, a route that had been well traveled at some point, although it was weedy and overgrown now. Thor got a thoughtful look and turned back, heading upriver again, but this time following the tracks. The trail angled up the hillside, doubling back once, still in deep woods. It ended in a flattened draw, edged with fallen trees and piled-up firewood, grey and peeling, branches and debris.

Thor kicked through the weeds near the back of the site, and let out a laugh. When he stamped the ground, she heard a hollow thump.

"It's here!" he said, dropping to his knees.

She crouched beside him as he cleared away detritus. It looked like a natural scattering of branches and needles, but he soon uncovered a metal hatch cover just like the one under the trailer. This hatch was unlocked. He hauled it open, revealing a square of darkness.

"It's not too deep," he said, "but my dad would've used his ladder to get in and out. Stay up here for now. Do you mind? You might have to throw down some wood for me to climb up on."

"I don't mind."

He swung his legs into the hole, which was wide enough for a man to fit through. When he landed, his face was still in light; it wasn't much deeper than he was tall. He crouched out of sight, and suddenly the hole filled with light. Kayla lay down and put her head through the opening, hanging partway down to look around. It was a small storeroom, maybe six by six. Wooden shelves, assembled in place, were wedged into the walls. They held few objects. Survival gear maybe? Water bottles, canned food, some tools, batteries. It looked like the remains of an emergency preparation kit, like one Chuck had stored in his garage. But there were also small wooden carvings, like miniatures of the hewn trees along the river. People and animals, stacked and squeezed together. The men resembled fish with hooked jaws and bulging eyes; the fish clasped long-fingered hands across their bellies, and perched on the men with finny feet.

"My dad must've made these," he said.

"I bet he wouldn't mind if you took one," she said. "To remember him by."

"Remember him for what?" he asked, flustering her. Had she said too much? Had she admitted knowledge he didn't have? He wasn't supposed to know his father was in jail. But there was nothing in what she had blurted, not really. She was nervous and wanted to protect him.

"No," he said. "No, I better leave it. And these...He must have been helping my uncles. I thought so, but I wasn't sure."

He touched a row of tall, narrow, rectangular cans with threaded caps.

"Is that paint thinner?"

"Black powder. Explosives. Don't worry, they're safe here. You'd need a fuse to set them off." He fumbled around on the shelves and came up with a length of black cord. "Like this one," he said. "You'd have to unscrew a cap and stick this in. Then if you lit it..."

He was showing off now, she realized.

"Thor...Thor!"

He blinked, and it was as if he suddenly realized how this must have looked to her.

"I have to get back," Kayla said. "My mom's going to be home from work soon, if she isn't already. I don't want her to come looking for me."

"Yeah, she'd get my gramma riled up and then my uncles'd come after us. I'm just happy we found this place. It's another sign, Kayla. When you're with me, good things happen."

When the hatch was shut, he kicked dirt and stones over it, trying to restore the site to its previous condition.

"My uncles wouldn't care if I'd found this place, but I can't have them thinking you might know about it. Like I said, my cousins from Fort Clark, they've been coming in and out with jeeploads of stuff under tarps. I don't know what all it is. They won't even tell me, and I'm family. They really don't trust outsiders. But…But I trust you, Kayla. I know if something happened to me, you…you'd help me out."

"Like what? Of course I would, I mean, but like what?"

He looked extra pale in the deep shade, his eyes huge from the darkness of the chamber.

"Nothing," he said. "You're the one for me, that's all."

He squeezed her hands, and they drew together for a long embrace before heading back down to the river's edge. They kept near the water to avoid running into his family. Haste was more important than staying unseen now that they were away from the dam. It struck her as odd that none of his uncles were ever down at the water, fishing in the pools. They seemed like the type that would be hunting and fishing every chance they got. Maybe they were more pure than the natives had been—the Indians with their ceremonies honoring the blessings of rich salmon runs that had sustained them for millennia. Maybe Thor's people were purer than that; they didn't eat the fish, only preserved and protected the stock. That struck her as incredibly noble and selfless and disciplined. Everything about Thor seemed to pull her toward a deeper understanding of nature, a greater truth unlike any she had ever imagined or believed in.

5

"Your mother and I don't want you hanging around with that boy. Those people. Any of them."

Chuck said this as they were driving up the hill to the bus stop the next morning.

"Your mother doesn't want to say it 'cause she thinks it would upset you and you're already so mad at her."

"I'm not mad at her," she said. "Don't put words in my mouth, Chuck."

"Don't talk to me like that."

"Why are you talking to me at all? You're not my father!"

"No, I'm not. I'm still fucking *alive!*"

She was shocked into silence. Chuck went white, his lips clenched tight as he stopped at the top of the hill. "Kayla... I'm sorry."

She flung the door open and threw her pack out onto the roadside, jumping down after it, then slammed the door and turned her back on the truck.

"Kayla..."

She didn't respond. His voice was muffled and he lowered the passenger window to call her name a few more times, but she wouldn't turn and let him see that she was fighting to keep from crying. He couldn't make her cry—not him.

"I'm sorry, Kayla. That didn't come out right. All I meant was, your mom and I—"

"Just leave me alone!" she said, and after a minute the truck groaned and moved off slowly down the road, around the curve. Its sulfurous brown exhaust thinned into the morning mist, and then the sound of its engine was replaced by the approaching rumble of the school bus. She heard tires squeal as it slowed at the sharp curve, just out of sight. It would appear any minute now, just where Chuck's truck had vanished.

At the last moment before it appeared, she kicked her backpack over the side of the road. It tumbled between the trees, gathering speed as it crashed through ferns and brambles. She followed it with little caution, skidding down the mulchy hillside, almost out of control and off balance, soil and humus filling her shoes, blackberry vines snagging her sweater and scratching up her hands.

She caught a tree and clung to it, hearing the bus screech to a stop. The weary engine idled on the roadside overhead for what seemed an eternity. Finally it heaved itself out of the turnaround and drove back toward town without her.

She supposed Thor must have some kind of homeschool schedule. She didn't want to get him in trouble. Besides, if her mom wanted to keep her away from Thor, she could only imagine Thor's grandmother felt the same way about her. But Kayla's curiosity was great. She had to admit that even before the fight with Chuck, she had been looking for a way to skip school and spend the day with Thor. She had never had a boyfriend. The sense of secrecy excited her. Had she made the fight with Chuck happen? Had she helped it along? Had she manufactured this excuse to justify slipping away? Well, so what? There was nothing at school that she needed to learn. She had no friends, nobody who cared about her except as a checkmark on an attendance sheet, necessary only so that the school could collect whatever the government paid it for her presence. Life went into limbo during school hours.

Whatever Thor's schooling was like, it had to be freer than hers. He had the whole of the woods and the river to take him in when he wasn't at his studies. She wondered what it would take to convince her mom that homeschool was the right approach for her as well. Maybe she and Thor could school together. Maybe with enough truancies, she would be expelled, and then her mother would be forced to homeschool her. She had thought the kids who homeschooled were weird or sick or antisocial, or did it because of strange religious beliefs that couldn't stand up to public scrutiny. But she was starting to see how wrong she had been.

Unlike any other kids she knew, Thor had principles. He was passionate about them. His family's truth was stronger than the one they forced on you when you were stuck in a classroom all day. What they taught in school had been bought and paid for by the government. She'd never seen it that way before meeting Thor. Of course, she'd been taught to believe what the government wanted her to think. Like the dam, for instance. The thought that a river could be dammed, with all the life in it stopped up and stunted, just so people could support overgrown cities and pollute even more rivers... Why accept that things had to be this way?

Thor had her questioning everything. He at least had been taught to think for himself. How special she had felt, when on his own he told her, "You're the one for me." So passionate, honest, wise, and free. *"You're the one for me."* How stupid she had been to think she could rescue *him* from anything. He was rescuing her, lifting her up from a life she hadn't realized held traps at every level.

At the bottom of the slope she found herself among large slabs of rock, tilted as if, like Kayla, they had just slid to the bottom of the hill. Between the rocks were crannies enough to hide her pack and keep her books dry if it rained. She moved along one stone face and heard a sound out of context—glass crunching underfoot. Looking down, she saw a chunk of safety glass, starred and shattered, little blue-green wedges of the stuff scattered on the soil. There was a crack in the rocks big enough to hold her pack; she shoved it in, well hidden. As she withdrew her arm, she spied a silver hoop amid the gleam of glass around her feet.

She stooped and slipped her finger through a key ring, rising to let it dangle as she inspected it. It held only a few keys. One might have been a house key, one was definitely a car key, and one was smaller than the rest: a padlock key.

Breathless, she stuffed the key ring into her pocket and moved off through the woods, angling toward the trailer, listening for voices all the while. It wasn't long before she heard them.

A house appeared through the trees, a small place with blistered green walls. No larger than a cabin, but lacking a cabin's charm. A hutch full of cowering rabbits was set against the back wall of the house, between coils of ribbed plastic tubing, chicken wire bales and salvaged boards, and faded bags of concrete that had hardened into their ultimate form. Beyond the house was an assortment of three-wheelers, tractors, and motorcycles, all in states of progressive decay that made it hard to tell if they had been driven here or dropped from the air. The voices she'd been hearing came from inside the house.

Before moving closer, she checked the woods to all sides. Upriver, she could barely make out another shack, this one a pale orange color, although it was so green with moss and mold it resembled one of the dying salmon on the riverbank. Beyond that place, in deeper woods, she glimpsed a dark wooden structure. Hammering sounded in the distance, followed by the barking of a dog that might have been Gompers.

No movement, no one else near. She crept to the corner of the house nearest the river, then sidled around to a window and peered inside.

Thor sat at a table eating a bowl of cereal. His grandmother stood at the stove, pouring steam from an enamel kettle into a metal cup, then turning toward Thor. Kayla fought repulsion. The grotesque old woman wore a ragged olive bathrobe that flapped open as she moved, revealing flat breasts with pale tips, almost nippleless, and rolls of skin that looked stitched together up the middle of her belly, as if she'd been cut open and sewn up in a hurry.

Kayla could only stop staring when the woman closed the robe with her free hand and sat down opposite Thor. Kayla crouched with her back to the wall, shivering in the cold morning air. She could feel them talking, a low buzz vibrating into her flesh. Then came her own name! Thor said it brightly, half singing it, and her heart soared—but then crashed as Freya began to yell at him, in words loud enough to carry through the thin wall: "She's not meant for you. She is *not* one of us and you will *not* see any more of her! This is our time, Thor. Our time! Your father's gone now and it's up to you to do your part. I didn't raise a little race traitor and neither did any of us. You're talking about tainting the old stock. It will not be allowed!"

"But you're not from the old stock originally. I know about you. You came into this family, just like—just like she would."

"I was different. I was meant to be here. I was chosen."

"Well, what if I choose her?"

"We won't let you risk contamination."

"But Gramma—"

"This is too important. And I don't mean just for now—this run. What we do here is for all time, Thor. Haven't I told you? I have!

Well anyway...she won't be around here to make trouble soon enough. None of them will, when the river runs free and our people are back where they belong. There's no place for her here. She's trash, Thor. Trash! She's not worthy of you. She's sure as hell not one of ours."

Whatever Thor might have answered, a phone started ringing and cut him off. Although the woman's feelings came as no surprise, Kayla was still shocked to hear them spoken aloud. They hit her harder than Chuck's outburst concerning her father. It was as if the adults on both sides were conspiring to keep them apart. It was a conspiracy of adults, as if deep below the surface, they were all playing parts in the same scheme.

She wondered—couldn't help wondering, although it was selfish—if Thor would betray his principles, his family, for her—for the two of them. She had to believe that in his heart, Thor felt Kayla was more important than any amount of...of brainwashing. To think she had come close to believing in it herself. They were both fools, brought up to believe the words of the adults appointed to care for them. But maybe now that she had a glimmer of the truth, she could help him see it as well.

She raised her head just enough to peer through the kitchen window again. Thor was still at the table, head bowed. Freya was standing, talking quietly into an old wall phone, gripping a handful of curly cord. She hooked the phone back into its cradle and started walking toward the door.

Kayla ducked, moved quickly around the corner to the back of the house. From here she could make a short dash to the shelter of the trees, and even scramble back up to the road if she must.

On the far side of the house, a door opened. She heard boot steps in the distance, crunching through fallen branches and needles. Someone was tromping closer from the direction of the orange house. She caught a glimpse of hulking shoulders, bright blue eyes in a bald bullet head.

As she rushed toward the trees, another man came straight at her out of them—bald, blue-eyed, a twin of the first. Kayla froze, wheeled back toward the house in time to see Freya rounding the corner with her hideous bathrobe flapping, not to mention what lay under it.

"Don't let her get away!" she cried. "She knows! Thor won't confess it, but he could've told her everything!"

There were three men in all. She didn't try to run. "I don't know anything," she said in a hoarse whisper, too quiet to be heard. As the nearest took her arms and walked her back toward the house, Thor came out to stare at her, aghast.

"Let her go!" he cried.

"Better put her somewhere she can't interfere," Freya instructed. She rounded on her grandson. "Is this how you show your faith, boy? Bringing an outsider into our business?"

"She came to me. You always said the one for me would come."

"Oh, she's coming all right," the woman said. "How you could think a little bitch like this could be the one…Well, you're a fool, boy. A fool!"

"He didn't tell me anything," Kayla said. "We're just friends."

Freya's face seethed. "Have you got a place you can put her?" she asked the men.

"We'll come up with something," one of them said.

"Not near the trailer—that's close enough her folks could hear, and they already been there once. They'll check there first."

"That wasn't my dad," she said.

"And shut her up," Freya commanded. "It won't be for long, you little slut."

"Gramma!"

"Just till we've put things right. Won't be long at all."

Thor fell mute. She could see his mind working, scared but still thinking, and a little of her fear ebbed away. He would come up with a way to get her out of this. She just had to trust him and be brave. This was no more than she had expected. His family was bound to reject her at first. But as long as Thor stuck with her, nothing else mattered.

The three uncles, two of them bullet-headed, pink as twin babies, narrowed their eyes and hooked their mouths at her in weird, twisted snarls, their lips hard and bunched as if dragging on cigarettes, making pinched kisses at her. The third man was dressed in coveralls, his hair not shaved but neatly trimmed. It was some sort of uniform. She remembered what Thor had said about them working for the water company, in order to keep a close watch on the river. The clean-cut uncle gave the others a nod, seeing that they had things under control. The twins led Kayla past the orange house, past the brown shack, past more structures and sheds and vehicles, past the compound from which she had heard sawing and shooting.

The valley was busy this morning. Men were hauling stuff from the shacks, throwing boxes and gear into trucks as if packing for an exodus. The uncles led her to a windowless sheet-metal shed, deep in the trees with not a glimpse of river. They wrenched the door open, and she saw an oil-stained dirt floor, shelves covered with tools, at which her hopes lightened—until they started pulling everything off the shelves and dumping it outside the shed on the forest floor. The shed was soon emptied. They pulled the shelves from the walls and flung them out as well.

The uncles kept back a roll of silver duct tape and started cutting off sections with a hunting knife, treating her with surprising gentleness.

"Now don't raise a fuss, Missy. We wouldn't want Thor upset with us for hurting you." One of the twins slapped a piece of tape over her mouth and the other bound her hands behind her back, talking to her as he worked. "This won't be for long. We're all going free tonight. You included."

What that meant, she had plenty of time to ponder after they sat her down in a corner of the shed, pushed the doors shut, and latched them. They walked off talking quietly.

They had taped her ankles as well as her wrists, so she could only scrunch up against the rear of the shed. She tried beating her head against the wall to make a sound, but the first good thump drove a sharp metal point into the back of her scalp just behind her right ear. Stung by the pain, as bad as a hornet's spike, she pulled away from the wall and huddled to herself in the dark.

Hours passed with no change except in the heaviness of her thoughts. She felt the balance of the day like a set of scales, evening out at midday and slowly tipping into afternoon. The slow growth of dusk, weighted toward nightfall.

She believed it would be wise to save her strength. When Thor came for her, she would need it. And if he didn't come... She couldn't force herself to think beyond that possibility.

At some point, Chuck would get home and then her mother, and they would guess she was out in the woods. They would immediately assume she had gone off with Thor, against their wishes. They would be angry. But angry enough to go looking for her, to question Freya? She could picture her mother's disappointment and how Chuck would get righteously indignant and blame it all on her mother, saying she had spoiled Kayla, been too coddling and lax with discipline. She imagined her mother's dismay turning to fear and panic, and after that she had to suppress her own fright. It was better to keep her thoughts on Thor, for thinking of him gave her hope and lifted her spirits.

But at some point, after Thor didn't come and still didn't come, the dull pain behind her ear turned into an idea.

She was agile enough to get to her feet, in spite of her ankles being taped together. With her back to the rear wall of the shed, she moved around to where she had punctured herself. Feeling carefully along the rippled corrugations of the wall, she found the sharp tip of an overlong screw protruding where two sheet metal panels overlapped. It was as sharp as she had imagined. She turned and centered it between her wrists, then shoved her arms back so the screw could dig into the tape. It caught there and she began to saw her hands up and down, widening the hole the screw had made. The tip pulled out but that didn't matter; the metal wall held it firmly in place. Gradually it ripped through the thick duct tape. She worked her bindings up and down, and sooner than she would have thought possible, her wrists began to come apart. She welcomed the tearing pain as the tape tore from her skin. Her hands were free.

She pulled away the ragged strip, then peeled more carefully at the patch across her mouth. Her lips were chapped, and it shredded them, but she was keenly sensitive to how trivial that pain was now. Anything short of a disabling injury must be ignored. She couldn't let herself be slowed. She had gone from dreaming about how Thor would save her, to wondering how badly he might need her help.

The tape was off her ankles now. She still didn't hear anything outside to make her think they were standing guard or paying any attention at all to the helpless little girl in the shed. She meant nothing to them. They must have thought they had dealt with her. It was some consolation to think that they had never had to do this before. Thor's uncles had no idea what a poor prison the shed made.

Once she could push on the doors from within, a gap appeared and was easily widened. The darkness outside frightened her. How long had she wasted waiting for Thor to save her? He must be in serious trouble by now.

She listened hard. Distant sounds, muffled by the forest. She hoped whatever noise she made would be similarly muted. She backed up, then threw herself hard at the doors. They parted another inch. She saw a padlock and a latch, starting to twist from their brackets. Kayla hurled herself at the doors again, and this time the latch tore loose all at once. She went tumbling onto the earth.

She scrambled around the side of the shed before she'd even found her feet, and plunged back into darkness without wondering which was the right direction. If the uncles had heard the commotion, she wouldn't have much time to get away. But after a few minutes of fumbling her way through the dark, groping around the rough black columns of trees, clawing through the damp, papery raking of ferns, she still heard no sounds of interest or pursuit.

First, on the off chance of impossible luck, she pulled her phone out of her pocket and checked it. It gave a faint light but of course there was no signal. She typed a quick text to her mother, nothing more than "mom u there?"

A fat exclamation mark popped up, signaling the phone's inability to send.

"So," she promised the night. "I'll do it myself."

6

There were lights on inside the trailer. Outside, next to it, a generator grumbled. An electric porch light glowed, and the light leaking through the grimy windows was steady and bright, not like the battery lantern Thor had used. The whole place shifted and creaked, as if a heavy weight were moving around inside. Kayla crouched in the bushes, seeing a shape move past the door—a blur of olive, the rippling shadow of Thor's grandmother.

She had hoped the trailer would be empty. Oh well. There was another way to get to the hiding spot. Inside the moldy vehicle, Freya muttered to herself. She wasn't really talking, Kayla realized as she crept around the back of the trailer; it sounded more like reading aloud, reciting prayers in some tongue Kayla didn't know.

As the trailer rocked and squealed, she got down on her belly and crawled under it. Heavy feet tramped over her head. She groped at the weedy soil until, stretched out full, she felt metal. She traced the edge of the hatch until she found the padlock, caked with dirt. She pulled the key ring from her pocket, forming a prayer herself now, every clink of metal sounding like a hammer to her. By touch she fit the key into the lock; it felt gritty and wrong, and she feared it was hopeless. But then it slid in all the way. She gasped as the lock fell open, heavy in her hand.

She slid the bar of the lock out of the latch and laid it in the dirt, where it couldn't scrape against the hatch and make a sound. Braced on her elbows, she felt for the hinges, then pushed the hatch back. Near the end of its arc, it got away from her grasp and fell the last few inches with an exhausted thud. She waited to hear if the woman overhead would react—but the mumbling chant and the restless pacing went on and on.

Stale air breathed up, giving her an impression of the chamber she had opened. She figured it would be similar to the one they had found the day before. She took out her useless cellphone and lit it up. The faint glow revealed shelves, as expected, but these were crowded with gear. Water bottles, boxes full of food, and ammunition. And then there were guns. Many guns. They were laid out carefully, gleaming black and silver and grey—rifles and shotguns and pistols. Beyond that, she didn't know enough to identify them. The guns frightened her more than anything she had ever seen, and she wondered if she could bring herself to use them. What if she had to?

Right then, she spied something she *could* use, thanks to Thor. Her heart lightened. He had prepared her for this.

There was no ladder; it was tucked up inside the trailer. She did a gymnast's move, lowering herself in head first while clinging to the edge of the hatch, then unfolding as if coming down off a horizontal bar. She had to drop a foot or so—not far. She turned the phone on again and cast its light over the shelves till she found the rectangular cans she had seen from above. Next to them were black fuses, glossy and new.

Thor had not been bragging after all; he had been instructing her in the part she would play. Events had been flowing this way all along, relentless as the river. All that happened had helped bring them together. Fate. She felt not unafraid but far less so than before. She also felt a new sense of resolve. His family was crazy, hers was broken. But between the two of them, they could create something new, something that never had been on this earth.

Thor had done his part, but he was helpless now. It was all up to her.

She unscrewed the threaded cap from one of the cans. The light from her phone didn't reach very far into the opening. She poked a black fuse into the hole, feeling slight resistance; then, hoping it was the right thing to do, she screwed the cap back on, not too tight but trapping the fuse in place. Boxes of matches sat on the shelf next to boxes of bullets and bags of disposable plastic lighters. She tore open a packet and put a lighter in her pocket.

The array of weapons intimidated her; she had never fired so much as a paint gun. Thor's uncles would laugh at her if she came at them with a machine gun. But the can of black powder was simple and she trusted it. She hoped that threats would be enough, but if they weren't, she knew that she could light the fuse. It would cause a loud blast that would bring help from up and down the valley.

Extricating herself from the pit wasn't too hard. She stacked a few cases of canned food until her head was at ground height. She set the powder can outside the hole, then got her armpits onto the edge and hauled herself up. As she stretched out on the ground, she misjudged her movements and thumped her head hard on the bottom of the trailer.

She froze, cursing herself, as footsteps sounded overhead, moving fast. The door squealed open and the whole trailer tipped and sighed as it was relieved of a certain weight. Bare white feet and legs touched the earth, just out of Kayla's reach. She held her breath. She was sure she could outrun Freya, but the uncles were another matter. Plus, if she fled, she would be abandoning Thor, which was unthinkable.

"Gamma! Gams, come on!" The uncles were calling. They were nearer than she'd realized.

"You got my boy?"

"We got him good and ready! Just waiting on you!"

There was a thick, liquid chuckle, and then something like a soft dark skin was shed. The olive robe sloughed off around ankles swollen like sausage casings about to burst. Freya's feet moved away from the trailer, out of sight. The generator died and the rumbling that had muffled Kayla's actions was gone. The porch light faded a bit but then held steady; there was enough residual battery power to keep it from snuffing out completely, just when she wished for total dark. In the sudden stillness she heard Freya's footsteps crunching off toward the river.

Kayla scrambled out from under the trailer, keeping to the shadow cast by the porch light, but still feeling exposed. Voices filtered through the trees, mixed with the voice of the river. She moved toward the sounds, trying to plan but feeling plans were pointless. Ideas rose from within her, but each one evaporated as soon as it started to form; it was like trying to hold onto dreams.

The rutted tire path was hard to follow in the dark, but she figured Freya would have been going even more slowly, barefoot. She couldn't quite believe the fat woman wasn't still struggling along the path.

Up ahead, the water appeared—a sheet of pale grey gleaming in the night. It was hard to separate the voices from the sound of the river; words were like gravel rolling over sand, a swirling swish of eddies, of bubbles breaking, splashing onto stones. She lost her balance on a sharp-edged rock, coming down hard on the heel of her free hand. The stench of rotten salmon overpowered her. She must have landed in carrion. But as she crouched there, letting the shock of pain fade from her throbbing palm, she gazed across the river and realized she was able to see in the faint light from the sky. Out in the open, free of branches, the clouds held a trace of glow reflected from the surrounding towns, the nearby city lights. On a clear night, with only starlight to rely on, it would have been black as a cave down here. But she could see more than she might have expected.

What she saw was a river alive with bodies. Silver as fallen starlight, holding the river's power as a coiled spring contains pent-up energy, they leapt and splashed and slithered up, ever up, the river. They were huge, bigger than any salmon she had seen by day or found dead along the banks. They looked more like the giants hauled from ocean trenches. They wriggled and twisted and dug into the gravel beds, inching forward like large glimmering worms. She thought of giant newts or salamanders, more amphibian than fish. But there was barely light enough to make such distinctions, and in the formless struggle she even had trouble telling one creature from another. They seemed a solid mass, as if the river had reversed course and was trying to heave itself higher into the mountains, crawling bodily back to its source.

This was the noise she'd heard, rocks overturning, the grunt of endless labor, and a low murmur that couldn't be coming from the fish.

The sound of voices, almost a choir, came from just upriver, around the bend. From the pool where she and Thor had set the salmon free. This was just a stop along the way for the teeming mass of swimmers, but a favored stop. She heard laughter and voices upraised, calling out, crying forth praise ecstatically. Jubilant cries, as if from a church meeting held in mid-river. All this sound came from water so shockingly cold it felt like knives in your flesh, like shards of ice that cut so sharp they numbed where they pierced. And yet in the grey light of the underslung clouds, the pool was shown to be full of revelers, their naked bodies paddling against the current, caught in the eddies, pushing up against the rocky sides.

"She comes, she comes, she comes!" One voice lifted above the others. Kayla froze and crouched, puzzled by the welcome in the voice. But they weren't looking at her, huddled on the shore. The faces were turned to stare straight down the river.

She peered back toward the bend, now so thick with salmon that she couldn't see the rocks. The figures flung themselves and clawed across each other—clawed although salmon shouldn't have claws. They gnashed their hooked jaws into one another's flesh, dragging each other down, all for the slightest advantage.

"No, Gramma, please!"

Thor's voice cut through all the other sounds. It came from the pool. She stared fiercely, intent on finding him among the pallid forms. The uncles, their bald heads shining, were easy to spot, with their stout bodies warped by water, their limbs merged with skeins of captured starlight. Among them, centered, was the small skinny form of the boy—thin, white, and vulnerable. The sight of him was a knife going into her, colder than the water. But worse still was the thing bobbing next to him: the grandmother, huge and white and billowing, a jellyfish, a mass of gelatin, a frog, a slimy mass like slugs mating. She opened her arms and pulled Thor into them. And as she drew him in, she seemed to burst. Her belly parted down the middle, along that terrible seam, gaping like a pouchy mouth. The water filled with shimmering pearls of matter—milky globes, caught in the pool's vortex, twisted around Thor like a tornado that had claimed him for its eye. Freya laughed and pulled him to her bosom.

"The roe! The roe!" she shouted. "Ready for the milt, boy! Ready for the milt!"

She heard screaming. But no, it wasn't Thor; it was Kayla herself.

She held out the can of black powder and screamed again as she stepped forward: "Let him go!"

They shut up, staring in her direction. She realized they couldn't see her clearly, so in her other hand, she struck the lighter.

"I have a bomb!" she said. "Let him go or I'll set it off! I'll blow up everything unless you let him go!"

"Don't be a fool, girl! There's no stopping this with your little bomb when the whole place is about to go. Tonight the river runs wild, and we all swim free! Set off your little bomb and see who cares!"

Taking advantage of the distraction, Thor had started toward her. He was scrambling out of the pool, into the gravel shallows.

"Where you going, boy?" Freya shouted.

"I... I'm going with Kayla," he said. "She's the one for me."

"The one for you, boy—is come."

Thor, half risen, went rigid—staring past her down the river. Kayla felt the lighter go out in her hand. Her gaze followed his.

Among the swarming slimy things, one far larger than all the others powered around the bend. The dull cloud-shine gathered in vast globes on either side of its head; it cleared a path among the flopping, finny swimmers. It came on like a barge, towed against the current, water boiling around its gaping mouth and fanning from its gills.

Thor dropped to his knees as if struck in the head, his jaw working mutely. He was naked, and more than that, he was erect, his pale member sticking up out of white curls. Kayla took a step back, in spite of herself. The old woman's words were mixed with wretched laughter.

"That's right, girl—she's the one for him! Lay down the roe, mother! My boys bring the milt! Come to us, olden other! Fishwife! Teem with us! Sport with us! To us your ways are sacred always! Spawnsister, spawn! Tonight we plant our fry and let the river deepen to keep 'em safe!"

Kayla regained her footing and her determination. She wouldn't give up on Thor. She could be strong for him now, when he was vulnerable.

The uncles climbed up to pull him back into the pool. Thor was lithe and slippery and managed, just barely, to elude them. The gigantic silver salmon surged upriver. The pink men made another grab at their nephew, and they were not the only ones. Just below the surface, fat fish darted and twined and gripped fat Freya's mammaries with fingered fins. They pawed at her as if to nurse, spinning circles in the pool, as they sprayed with silvery milk the cloud of eggs she had released. Decayed in life, their purpose done, they mouthed her slack flesh, as Freya lolled back with spread limbs framing the raw gape of her opened belly. The salmon and their siblings nestled up between her thighs like koi swarming for handfuls of silver corn. Still other fish finned around the uncles, their scaly crowns strung with strands of stringy hair like riverweed, green with moss but blond beneath. They wrapped the uncles in their drowning locks, while the men made horrible moaning sounds but did not fight or struggle, as the queen of them all lumbered ever upriver, as Thor put out a skinny leg and started sliding back into the pool.

"No!" she screamed and lit the waxy fuse. The sputtering flame didn't make enough light to show anything more than the outline of her fingers clenched on the powder can. It was burning fast, and so she threw it. Into the center of the pool it dropped, lost with scarcely a splash among all that churning of skin and scales. She got both arms around Thor and hauled him back toward the trees, dragging him off balance. They tumbled to the stony bank together.

The first explosion was more a thing of pressure than of sound. She felt it in the rocks beneath their bodies. The pool became a huge, bright bubble of expanding liquid light, leaping from its bed. It was as if the river were turned inside out and exposed with an X-ray. She saw them all captured, frozen, suspended in the burst—the human limbs and the fins of fish, long spines and ribcages—suddenly fusing into a pulverized mash. The force of the blast was strong enough to undercut the opposite bank. She heard, as the water splashed down again, the collapse of the cliffside, a rush and rumble of earth, rock and timber. In the dim skyshine, it looked as if the hillside took a step forward and stomped down into the river. The mother of the fish was smothered in the avalanche, and all the swarming millions were entombed in an instant.

She was still watching the mound where the pool had been when the next explosion hit them—then the third—then more and more.

The booms came echoing down the canyon from far upriver. Now it was Thor's turn to be strong. He got to his feet and helped her up—half-carrying her, so her feet kicked at the air and seemed to glide over the trickiest patches of rock. They were moving downstream. The river still seethed with salmon, but Thor seemed to float, and she felt as if she weighed nothing. What was this sensation of release? Were they free? That must be it. Free as the river that even now surged black, unseen, and irresistible at their backs.

Thor knew where to turn and cut away from the bank. Ahead she saw the bright raw wood chalet, its sightless windows gazing at the river. It had never felt like home but still she was glad to see it. Beyond, strange lights swept through the trees, casting the house in and out of shadow. As they hurried around the side of the house, she saw a police car in the driveway. Next to it, her mother and Chuck were talking with two cops. One was talking urgently into his radio, staring upriver.

"The dam is going!" Kayla shouted, pulling Thor along with her, feeling him resist and knowing it was his nakedness that held him back. But that didn't matter now. This was her place, her time. She would protect him. "We have to go, the river's coming! The dam is down! They blew it up!"

Her mother's face was terrified and relieved, Chuck's expression startled and sour.

"It was my uncles," Thor confirmed. "They blew it up and it's coming down. Kayla's right, we have to get away."

Kayla ran to let Gompers out of his kennel, as Chuck jumped into his truck. "Get in!" he shouted.

The sirens had started. The cop car screeched away toward the cul de sac, throwing gravel, then pitching sharply into the neighboring drive. She heard the bullhorn squawk, and then the warning to evacuate. Car alarms were wailing. The valley filled with noise. Beneath it all was a deeper rumbling. The river was coming.

"Kayla," her mother said. "Oh, Thor, you poor boy!"

Scrawny and wet, he should have been blue with cold. Instead he seemed suddenly at ease, even confident. He helped Gompers into the back of the truck. Kayla held the door so they could both climb in.

Cold water swirled around her ankles. Things in the dark yard were starting to move, lawn chairs and abandoned tires, shifting and drifting away. The voice of the river was all around them, high and soft, hissing over the earth and through the trees.

"Kayla, get in!" her mother screamed.

"Thor," she said, "come on, you first."

"Come the fuck on!" Chuck shouted. The truck lurched forward; she had to grab the door before it swung shut. Down the road, at other houses, people were shouting. Jousting headlights swept across the cul de sac.

Kayla's mother leapt down from the truck and grabbed her with surprising strength, pulling her daughter in beside her. Thor's cold fingers slid from her grasp, and he made no move to follow.

In the red glare of the taillights, she saw that he'd been held back by other hands. Thin, bony, white membranous fingers were wrapped around his calves. Arms beckoned up from the swirling torrent, trying to pull him down. His expression was dreamy with longing. He showed no sign of wanting to resist.

He looked up at Kayla, met her eyes, and nodded, silently promising that he would be all right. Promising whatever she wanted.

The door slammed. The truck roared and sloshed toward the road. Once it stalled, but Chuck gunned the engine. They cut out in front of the cop car and veered onto concrete, gaining ground on the steep road up out of the valley. They climbed fast, leaving the floodwaters below, and were well clear when the dam gave way completely and everything in the river's course was swept away.

Kayla thought of Thor as she had last seen him. The hands reaching up to pull him under. Thor joining gladly with the others. Willingly bowing, kneeling, lowering himself into the water before it could sweep him away.

She fixed her mind on the promise she'd seen in his eyes and felt in her heart, the only hope that still remained to her, tantamount to certainty.

He would return. To this river, this valley, to what remained of their pool.

If not next year, then the year after that, or the year after that.

He would return.

And so would she.